Samuel French Acting Edition

I0591800

Curvy Widow

Book by
Bobby Goldman

Music & Lyrics by
Drew Brody

SAMUELFRENCH.COM   SAMUELFRENCH.CO.UK

FOR PRODUCTION ENQUIRIES

UNITED STATES AND CANADA
Info@SamuelFrench.com
1-866-598-8449

UNITED KINGDOM AND EUROPE
Plays@SamuelFrench.co.uk
020-7255-4302

Each title is subject to availability from Samuel French, depending
upon country of performance. Please be aware that *CURVY WIDOW*
may not be licensed by Samuel French in your territory. Professional
and amateur producers should contact the nearest Samuel French
office or licensing partner to verify availability.

MUSIC USE NOTE

Licensees are solely responsible for obtaining formal written permission from copyright owners to use copyrighted music in the performance of this play and are strongly cautioned to do so. If no such permission is obtained by the licensee, then the licensee must use only original music that the licensee owns and controls. Licensees are solely responsible and liable for all music clearances and shall indemnify the copyright owners of the play(s) and their licensing agent, Samuel French, against any costs, expenses, losses and liabilities arising from the use of music by licensees. Please contact the appropriate music licensing authority in your territory for the rights to any incidental music.

IMPORTANT BILLING AND CREDIT REQUIREMENTS

If you have obtained performance rights to this title, please refer to your licensing agreement for important billing and credit requirements.

CURVY WIDOW premiered in New York City at the Westside Theatre on August 3, 2017. The performance was directed by Peter Flynn, with choreography by Marcos Santana, scenic design by Rob Bissinger, costume design by Brian Hemesath, lighting design by Matthew Richards, and sound design by Ryan Rumery and M. Florian Staab. The production stage manager was CJ LaRoche. The cast was as follows:

BOBBY	Nancy Opel
JIM	Ken Land
CAROLINE	Andrea Bianchi
HEIDI	Elizabeth Ward Land
JOAN	Aisha De Haas
SHRINK	Alan Muraoka
PER SE	Christopher Shyer

CHARACTERS

BOBBY
JIM
CAROLINE
HEIDI
JOAN
SHRINK
PER SE
OTHERS

SETTING

New York City

TIME

The present

Scene One: Jim and Bobby's Fifth Avenue Apartment

(There is no curtain at open. A man and a woman are sleeping. The woman is **BOBBY**. *She is in her mid-fifties with short, salt and pepper hair. As the lights come up and the music begins, she bolts upright in the bed, followed by the alarm clock going off. The man is her husband,* **JIM**. *He is much older, distinguished, and grey-haired. He slowly gets out of bed and puts on an ornate silk robe as* **BOBBY** *starts to get dressed and sings.)*

[MUSIC NO. 01 "UNDER CONTROL"]

BOBBY.
JUMPING OUT OF BED IT'S
TIME TO START THE DAY
DON'T NEED AN ALARM CLOCK
WHO SLEEPS ANYWAY?
THERE'S TOO MUCH TO GET DONE
BUT I WILL FIND A WAY
I'VE GOT IT UNDER CONTROL

(Fully dressed, rummaging through her purse.) Jim did you sign the Warner's contract?

JIM. I can't, I couldn't find my blue pen.

BOBBY. Maybe live a little and use the black one?

JIM. *(Shakes his head.)* Bad luck.

BOBBY. Jimmy, please sign with another pen. I'm late for my meeting with my clients.

JIM. I need my blue pen.

BOBBY. Can I just forge your name with the black one?

JIM. Nope. You'd have to use the blue one.

*(The household **STAFF** enters, variously executing their morning duties.)*

BOBBY.

JIM'S AT HIS DESK, WRITING
A DEADLINE IMPENDS
I'M OFF TO A MEETING
WITH BRAND NEW CLIENTS
IN THE AFTERNOON
I'LL PREP FOR DINNER WITH MY FRIENDS
I'VE GOT IT UNDER CONTROL
UNDER CONTROL, UNDER CONTROL
WHATEVER IT TAKES I KEEP THINGS
UNDER CONTROL

*(The **STAFF** exits variously.)*

JUST A DAY IN THE LIFE OF A WIFE OF A WRITER
SPINNING PLATES, WITH FINGERS IN PIES
ME AND HIM, BOBBY AND JIM.
THAT'S OUR LIVES, TWO HALVES MAKE A WHOLE
EVERYTHING'S UNDER CONTROL

*(Various **PEOPLE** from Bobby and Jim's life enter. **BOBBY** is on the phone interacting with each of them.)*

CLIENT.

MY KITCHEN SINK EXPLODED

AGENT.

WILL YOU OK THE DEAL?

PUBLISHER.

HAS JIM FINISHED HIS REWRITES?

STUDIO EXEC.

TELL JIM THE SCRIPT NEEDS SEX APPEAL

FRIEND.

OF COURSE I'LL BRING THE WINE SINCE YOU
ALWAYS MAKE THE MEAL

BOBBY.

YEAH YEAH YEAH – UNDER CONTROL

ENSEMBLE.

UNDER CONTROL, UNDER CONTROL

BOBBY.

> THROW WHAT YOU WANT AT ME
> I'LL GET IT UNDER CONTROL

ENSEMBLE.

> JUST A DAY IN THE LIFE OF A WIFE OF A WRITER
> PUTTING OUT FIRES AND JUGGLING KNIVES

BOBBY.

> ME AND HIM

ENSEMBLE.

> BOBBY AND JIM. THAT'S THE TEAM, EYES ON THE GOAL

JIM. *(Entering from his office.)* It's pouring outside.

BOBBY. I have just the thing.

> *(She hands him an elaborate umbrella with a bow on it.)*

JIM. It's the cherry briar one I saw at Christie's.

BOBBY. *(Smiles.)* I thought it would make you happy.

JIM. *(Stroking umbrella.)* She's a thing of beauty. Thanks, Bobby.

> **(BOBBY** *gives him a kiss as* **JIM** *exits.)*

ENSEMBLE.

> TO HAVE AND TO HOLD
> FOR BETTER OR WORSE

BOBBY.

> IT'S THE VOW THAT YOU MAKE FROM THE START

ENSEMBLE.

> FOR RICHER OR POORER, IN SICKNESS AND HEALTH

BOBBY.

> TILL DEATH DO YOU PART

ENSEMBLE.

> TILL DEATH DO YOU, DEATH DO YOU, DEATH DO YOU
> DEATH DO YOU PART

> *(Music stops.* **ENSEMBLE** *freezes as music begins again slowly.)*

> NOT IN CONTROL
> NOT IN CONTROL
> SUDDENLY LIFE MAKES IT CLEAR THAT YOU'RE

NOT IN CONTROL
JUST A DAY IN THE DEATH OF A WORLD-FAMOUS
WRITER

BOBBY.

BLINK AN EYE
SNAP

ENSEMBLE. Gasp!

BOBBY.

AND HE'S GONE

ENSEMBLE.

LIGHTS DIM ON BOBBY AND JIM.

BOBBY.	**ENSEMBLE.**
LEFT BEHIND – A HALF	OOH
AND A HOLE	

(Music resumes original tempo.)

BOBBY & CLIENT.

GET IT UNDER CONTROL

FRIEND, PUBLISHER, AGENT & STUDIO EXEC.

FACING THE PRIME OF YOUR LIFE AS A WIDOW
FACING THE WORLD ALL ON YOUR OWN

BOBBY & CLIENT.

UNDER CONTROL

FRIEND, PUBLISHER, AGENT & STUDIO EXEC.

FIGURE IT OUT LITTLE BY LITTLE

ENSEMBLE.

ONE DAY AT A TIME

ENSEMBLE & BOBBY.

YOU TRY

BOBBY.

TO KEEP IT UNDER CONTROL

ENSEMBLE.

A CHANGE IN THE LIFE OF A WIFE OF A WRITER
OVER THE EDGE

ENSEMBLE & BOBBY.

KEEP IT UNDER CONTROL

(Scene transition: two male **MOURNERS** *come to* **BOBBY** *to pay their respects. As they finish,* **BOBBY** *crosses into...)*

[MUSIC NO. 01A "AFTER CONTROL – INSTRUMENTAL"]

Scene Two: Living Room in Bobby's Apartment

> (**BOBBY** *is on her couch. Each of her friends enters.* **CAROLINE** *is mid-fifties, a CFO, and married to a doctor.* **HEIDI** *is single in a VP position.* **JOAN** *is also single and a small-business owner. They are all smart and funny enough with each other to be long-time friends.*)

CAROLINE. *(Pressing a medicine bottle into* **BOBBY**'s *hand.)* I stole these from my husband. The perks of being married to a doctor. They're great for sleep.

HEIDI. *(Giving* **BOBBY** *a pill bottle.)* And take these for anxiety. God knows you're going to have enough of it. Besides they will help you sleep.

JOAN. *(Offering two different pill bottles.)* Now – these are for depression and these are for sleep.

> *(Taking them back.)*

What am I doing? I'm always depressed and I never sleep.

CAROLINE. *(Looking around.)* Is the family still pretending you're not Mrs. Goldman?

BOBBY. Thirty years and counting. They're going for a record.

CAROLINE. I'm sorry.

HEIDI. Are you planning any kind of service?

BOBBY. No, Jim would have hated that. Just a simple cremation. As little fuss as possible.

CAROLINE. When I die I just want to be dropped in front of the door at Hermes. Heidi what about you?

HEIDI. Stuffed and mounted so my husband can mourn me. Forever.

JOAN. Well I'm not paying Campbell's. That funeral home starts in the stratosphere and goes up to ridiculous.

BOBBY. Everything is à la carte.

HEIDI. Use your AMEX.

BOBBY. You mean I could get miles?

JOAN.	CAROLINE.	HEIDI.
Yeah!	Why not?	Of course!

BOBBY. I almost forgot, Peter Luger sent steaks.

JOAN. *(Starts to exit toward kitchen.)* Luger steaks? Then why are we talking to you instead of eating?

BOBBY. That's why we're friends.

HEIDI. *(Starts to exit with* **JOAN.***)* I'll fix you a plate.

BOBBY. Not hungry.

(All three **WOMEN** *stop in their tracks.)*

HEIDI. That settles it. If you are not hungry, then you definitely can't deal with this on your own.

BOBBY. Of course I can. I have my construction company and I'll still have to make all of Jim's deals, manage his works, you know...

JOAN. Just throw in a root canal and a high colonic, and you're all set.

CAROLINE. Can't you for once just respect something stupid that Bobby says? After all, we're here to comfort her. Now don't you worry about a thing. We are here for you.

JOAN. *(Exiting to the kitchen.)* Don't count on me. Anyone else want champagne?

CAROLINE. *(Following* **JOAN.***)* Joan, why is champagne your answer to everything?

HEIDI. Bobby, you've got to eat something. What do you want?

BOBBY. I'm not sure.

HEIDI. I'll take care of you.

*(***HEIDI** *exits.* **BOBBY** *is alone onstage.)*

[MUSIC NO. 02 "TURN THE PAGE"]

BOBBY.
DO I DRINK COFFEE?
DO I EAT FRUIT?

DO I LIKE TAKING WALKS ON A WHIM?
WELL I DID WITH HIM

HE LIKED THE SUN
SUN EVERYWHERE
IN DECEMBER OUR LIVING ROOM
LIKE ARIZONA AT HIGH NOON

I PREFER TO LIVE LIKE A BAT IN A CAVE
DRAW THE SHADES
MAKE THEM BLACKOUT
BACK OUTSIDE WHERE SUN SHOULD STAY
STAY AWAY
NOW I CAN SAFELY SAY
I PREFER THE DARK

HALF A LIFE AND HE'S ALL I'VE EVER KNOWN
HALF A LIFE AND TONIGHT I EAT ALONE
SLOW IT DOWN, CAN I CATCH MY BREATH?
IS IT TIME TO MAKE CHOICES YET?
START AGAIN AT MY AGE?
CHAPTER END, TURN THE PAGE

THIS APARTMENT'S MINE
THIS ROOM IS MINE
THIS TABLE'S MINE,
THESE CLOTHES ARE MINE!
THIS CHAIR IS MINE

DO I LIKE THIS CHAIR?
HIS FAVORITE CHAIR?
HIS TREASURED CHAIR,
THIS CHAIR HE CARED ABOUT SO MUCH
THIS CHAIR JUST SITTING THERE
STARING AT ME
CHAIRING AT ME
DARING ME "BOBBY,
GO AHEAD AND THROW ME OUT"

I HAVE NO DOUBT
I HATE THIS CHAIR

HALF A LIFE AND HE'S ALL I'VE EVER KNOWN
HALF A LIFE AND TONIGHT I SLEEP ALONE

IN THE BED WE SHARED ALL THESE YEARS
THROUGH THE FIGHTS –
THROUGH THE LAUGHTER AND TEARS
ALL THE JOY, ALL THE RAGE
CHAPTER END, TURN THE PAGE

LOOKING AROUND
I'M COMPLETELY SURROUNDED BY MEMORIES
NOW IT FEELS WRONG
DO I EVEN BELONG HERE ANYWAY?

I DID.

FOR HALF A LIFE
FOR HALF A LIFE
SLOW IT DOWN, CAN I CATCH MY BREATH?
IS IT TIME TO MAKE CHOICES YET?
IF I HAVE TO BE JUST ME
WILL I EVEN KNOW HOW?
I'M BREATHING – WHAT NOW?

DO I DRINK COFFEE?
DO I EAT FRUIT?

HALF A LIFE AND CHANGE
CHAPTER END, TURN THE PAGE

(**BOBBY** *turns off the lights and exits.*)

(*Scene transition: the shrink's office appears with a* **MARRIED COUPLE** *finishing their session. They exit as* **BOBBY** *enters to…*)

[MUSIC NO. 02A "SHRINK WRAP"]

Scene Three: Shrink's Office

(The room contains a couch and a couple of big chairs.)

BOBBY. So I'm finally meeting the shrink we've been paying for the last umpteen years. Did Jim sit in the chair or lay on the couch?

SHRINK. *(Smiling.)* Do you feel uncomfortable seeing me?

BOBBY. You mean because you've spent years listening to Jim tell you all our secrets?

> *(SHRINK laughs and shrugs, BOBBY lies down on couch. SHRINK sits.)*

I just don't like to waste time. I figure you know the backstory.

SHRINK. That's very practical.

BOBBY. It's one of my virtues. Besides I'm only here to shut my friends up. I say I can handle a little death.

SHRINK. Bobby, you were married over thirty years. You've been robbed of your husband. Your life is completely changed.

BOBBY. *(Angrily.)* Don't I know that? We did everything together. His friends were my friends. His interests were my...

> *(She starts to cry. SHRINK hands her a Kleenex box.)*

(Stopping herself.) I'm fine. I'm fine. Just a weak moment.

SHRINK. Do you think it's okay to cry?

BOBBY. Yes but it's been months now. It's time to...

SHRINK. Feel in charge?

> *(BOBBY nods and cries softly.)*

Being in control may be overrated. Maybe there is a certain satisfaction throwing everything in the air?

BOBBY. Hasn't my life been upended enough?

SHRINK. Have you ever tried just letting go?

BOBBY. Once. What a disaster.

SHRINK. Do me a favor.

(**BOBBY** *stands and follows his instructions.*)

[MUSIC NO. 03 "WHITE BOX LOFT"]

(*Underscored and spoken.*) Close your eyes. Take a breath. Good. Drop your hands. Now picture yourself standing in a room. And imagine you're happy in this room, in this space. It feels comfortable. It can be anywhere you want, any place at all. Now tell me – what do you see?

(*As she sings,* **BOBBY** *moves away from the shrink's office. Throughout the song, the stage transforms into Bobby's new downtown loft apartment. It's a cool, sophisticated New York space. It's sexy and slightly masculine, very different from the Fifth Avenue apartment.*)

BOBBY.

IT'S A WHITE BOX LOFT
JUST FOUR CLEAN WALLS
AND I'M STANDING IN THE CENTER
WITH MY HARD HAT
IN A WHITE BOX LOFT
JUST AN EMPTY ROOM
AND IT'S NOWHERE NEAR FIFTH AVENUE

(*The* **MOVING COMPANY** *enters.*)

ENSEMBLE.

GOODBYE, GOODBYE

BOBBY.

TO STUFFY PENTHOUSE LIFE

ENSEMBLE.

GOODBYE

BOBBY.

TO FORMAL DINNERS EVERY NIGHT
I'M HAPPILY LEAVING THE WORLD OF

CHANEL SUITS BEHIND
ENSEMBLE.
GOODBYE, GOODBYE

(The **MOVING COMPANY** *exits variously.)*

BOBBY.
TO ALL THOSE PRYING EYES
ALL OVER THE UPPER EAST SIDE
WHERE EVERYWHERE I GO
I SEE EVERYONE I KNOW　　　**ENSEMBLE.**
LET GO. PUT THE PAST　　　OOOH...
OUT TO PASTURE
I'M MOVING DOWNTOWN

(The **CONSTRUCTION/CONTRACTING COMPANY**
*enters and exits variously throughout the rest
of the number.)*

ENSEMBLE.
WEEK ONE
CARPENTER 1.
RUN ELECTRICITY
CARPENTER 2.
FRAME THE WALLS WHERE THEY WILL BE
BOBBY.
AS I LEARN THE INS AND OUTS OF BUSY STREETS.
ENSEMBLE.
WEEK THREE
CARPENTER 1.
DRYWALL AND PLASTERING
CARPENTER 2.
PLUMBING, HEAT AND SANDBLASTING
BOBBY.
FIND MY PLACES TO GRAB COFFEE
AND MY FAVORITE SPOTS TO EAT
ENSEMBLE.
WEEK FIVE

CARPENTER 1.

LAY THE FLOOR

BOBBY.

MEET MY NEIGHBORS

> *(Music stops as **BOBBY** greets her artsy bohemian **NEIGHBOR**.)*

Hi. I'm, Mrs. Gold–

> *(A beat.)*

Nice to meet you, I'm Bobby.

NEIGHBOR. *(Indifferent.)* 'Sup.

> *(He makes a fist and raises it. She reacts but then realizes he's only trying to fist bump. She returns the fist bump.)*

> *(Music continues.)*

BOBBY.

LIFE'S DIFFERENT DOWNTOWN

ENSEMBLE.

DOES IT FEEL LIKE FREEDOM, BOBBY?

DOES IT FEEL LIKE STARTING FRESH?

NOW YOU'VE GONE AND THROWN YOUR LIFE UP

IN THE AIR

BOBBY.

WELL THERE'S ROOM FOR THINGS TO HAPPEN

AND ROOM TO SPARE

ENSEMBLE.

SOME SPACE TO MAKE MISTAKES

WEEK SIX

PROJECT MANAGER.

ADD PAINT AND FURNITURE

CARPENTER 2.

FIXTURES, HARDWARE, RUGS AND DOORS

BOBBY.

AND MY BRAND-NEW LEATHER JACKET SUITS ME FINE

ENSEMBLE.

WEEK NINE

BOBBY.

> INVITE MY GIRLFRIENDS
> THEY CAN HARDLY COMPREHEND
> THEY'RE TAKEN BY SURPRISE

GIRLFRIENDS.

> WE CAN'T BELIEVE OUR EYES!

BOBBY.

> WEEK TEN AND I SLEEP IN MY NEW BED
> I SLEEP BETTER DOWNTOWN

ENSEMBLE.

> FROM A WHITE BOX LOFT
> WITH FOUR BLANK WALLS

BOBBY.

> NOW I'M WAKING UP AND MAKING NEW DECISIONS
> IN MY DOWNTOWN LOFT

ENSEMBLE.

> WITH NO UPTOWN RULES

BOBBY.

> I'M OPENING THE DOORS

ENSEMBLE.

> OPENING THE DOORS

BOBBY.

> AND READY TO EXPLORE

ENSEMBLE.   **BOBBY.**

> READY FOR WHATEVER'S   WHO KNOWS WHAT'S IN
>   IN STORE   STORE?

BOBBY.

> FEELS LIKE MY OWN

BOBBY & ENSEMBLE.

> FEELS LIKE HOME

[MUSIC NO. 03A "LOFTY DESIRES"]

Scene Four: Shrink's Office

SHRINK. I haven't seen you in quite a while.

BOBBY. Sorry. You can't imagine the change: I'm finally living life among the young and the hip instead of the old and the hipless.

SHRINK. How do you like the new apartment?

BOBBY. *(Pacing around.)* It makes me happy. Really happy. Do you know I have a twenty-four-hour diner a block away?

> *(She goes into her pocketbook and takes out a lamb chop from a baggie and starts gnawing on it.)*

There are people everywhere all the time. Where we used to live everyone went away for the summer. If you collapsed on the street during July no one would find your body till after Labor Day.

> *(She takes another bite so the bone is hanging out of her mouth.)*

SHRINK. *(Indicating the lamb chop.)* Is that a lamb chop?

BOBBY. *(As she polishes off the chop.)* This was left over from breakfast. I'm eating everything in sight. I swear I would eat your sweater if it wouldn't make me cough up a hairball.

SHRINK. *(Laughs.)* Maybe the eating is really something else? And you're stuffing your face instead of stuffing your...?

BOBBY. *(Interrupting.)* Do you have any snacks in your office?

SHRINK. Maybe it's time for you to have some male companionship? It might help fulfill some of the urges better than extra-large orders of French fries.

BOBBY. First of all, don't knock French fries. And of all the second-rate Freudian diagnoses...what's next? That my vagina is commanding my appetite?

SHRINK. Have you thought about going out with someone?

BOBBY. Absolutely not. Don't be ridiculous. Who would I go out with? I don't know any single men.

SHRINK. Don't you know anyone who can fix you up?

BOBBY. I know everyone my girlfriends know. So what's the point?

SHRINK. Have you heard of Match.com?

BOBBY. You must be kidding.

SHRINK. I think you need to be jump-started. Many of my patients have tried Match.

BOBBY. Just go out with anybody? I can't do that. I've never been with another man since I got married.

SHRINK. I think you need this. I'm making getting laid a medical directive.

BOBBY. Can you do that?

> *(Scene transition: **BOBBY** crosses the stage as it transforms back to...)*

Scene Five: Bobby's Loft

[MUSIC NO. 03B "GET LAID"]

(**BOBBY** *is in her new bedroom, pacing.*)

BOBBY. *(To audience.)* Go online for a pick-up? The shrink has lost his mind. He should be the one on the couch.

(*The* **ENSEMBLE** *enters, voicing her unconscious.*)

ENSEMBLE.
GET LAID, LAID. GET LAID, LAID.

BOBBY. *(Goes to computer.)* What a fall from grace. I was a Fairfield County princess. I jumped horses. I showed poodles.

ENSEMBLE.
GET LAID, LAID. GET LAID, LAID.
YEAH!

(*The* **ENSEMBLE** *exits, giggling.* **BOBBY** *grabs her laptop.*)

[MUSIC NO. 04 "AGE/HEIGHT/WEIGHT"]

BOBBY.
LET'S JUST SAY FOR ARGUMENT'S SAKE
I DO THIS THING MY SHRINK THINKS I SHOULD DO
LET'S JUST SAY I OPEN THE SCREEN

(*She opens the screen.*)

I CHOOSE A SITE, I CHOOSE A NAME
I FIND A MAN WHO SAYS HE'S GAME
WHAT THEN? WHAT THEN?

DOES HE COME TO MY APARTMENT
DO I CLICK AND HE APPEARS?
OR DO WE CHOOSE A NEUTRAL SPOT
LIKE A HOTEL OR RESTAURANT
THE MIND REELS FROM THE DETAILS
AS I'M REELING OFF MY FEARS

LIKE: WHAT IF I HATE HIM?
WHAT IF HE HATES ME?

WHAT IF HE'S PSYCHO AND TOTALLY CRAZY?
WHAT IF HE'S A KILLER?
OR A HIPPIE?
OR A VEGAN?
GET LAID
NO WAY

BUT LET'S JUST SAY FOR ARGUMENT'S SAKE
I INVESTIGATE THIS DATING ON THE WEB
LIKE A SOCIOLOGIST MIGHT
OBSERVING THROUGH PARTICIPATION
ATTEMPTING INTERNET TEMPTATION
SEEKING DIGITAL RELATIONS
WORKING UP THE NERVE
TO GET WHAT I DESERVE
I MIGHT CATCH A CATCH, OR CATCH THE CLAP,
OR CATCH A TOTAL BOMB

AH WHAT THE HELL
LET'S CHECK OUT MATCH.COM.

Please take a few minutes to fill out your profile.
Profile? What's a profile? Oh I see. An ad.

Height – five foot six.

Weight – fuck off.

Eyes – green.

Hair – salt and pepper.

Age? – Prime of life.

Oh it needs a number –

THIRTY-EIGHT
FORTY-EIGHT
GODDAMMIT FIFTY-FIVE

Picture? No way. User name? Huh.

[MUSIC NO. 05 "CURVY WIDOW"]

FOR THE FIRST TIME IN MY LIFE
I CAN BE ANONYMOUS
EVERYONE HERE IS PSEUDONYMOUS
ALONE IN NEW YORK
JULIET NEEDS ROMEO
GODZILLA FOR MOTHRA

I NEED A HANDLE
THAT CONVEYS THE PERFECT MESSAGE
I NEED A HANDLE
THAT SPEAKS TO WHO I AM
AND AS LONG AS I'M INVENTING SOMEONE
BASICALLY FROM SCRATCH
WHY NOT SOMEONE SEXY
SOMEONE FUN
SOMEONE WHO ACTUALLY
DOESN'T GIVE A DAMN

BUT STILL IT'S GOTTA FIT ME
HOW ABOUT SEXUALLY STARVED IN THE CITY?
NEUROTIC IN MANHATTAN?
THAT WON'T ATTRACT 'EM
DEAD FAMOUS HUSBAND?
SURE, THEY'LL COME RUNNING

WHO AM I?
I'M A WIDOW
THAT'S NOT THE SAME AS SINGLE
WIDOW SAYS DESIRABLE
BUT STILL A LITTLE VULNERABLE, TOO
(AND MEN LIKE THAT)

RICH WIDOW? NO
SMART WIDOW? NO
I DON'T KNOW WHAT TO SAY WIDOW?
EVERY DAY MORE GREY WIDOW?
WAIT!
WHAT WOULD MY SEXY NEW PERSONA SAY?

SHE'D FOCUS ON HER ASSETS
SHE'D BE A BIT MORE NERVY
LET'S TAKE STOCK, BOOBS AND ASS – YES
HIPS – YES
I GUESS SHE'D SAY:
CURVY

HOW ABOUT CURVY WIDOW?
LOOK OUT, SHE'S GOT YOU IN HER SITES

CURVY WIDOW'S NOT ASHAMED
CURVY WIDOW'S NOT AFRAID

SHE WANTS WHAT SHE WANTS
AND SHE GETS WHAT SHE WANTS
'CAUSE SHE TAKES WHAT SHE WANTS
AND SHE WANTS TO GET LAID

CURVY WIDOW'S LICKING HER LIPS
SHE'S SHAKING HER HIPS
CURVY WIDOW'S GOT YOU IN HER SITES

(She goes to the computer and begins typing.)

DEAR WHOEVER YOU ARE
YOU SEEM INTERESTING
I'VE NEVER DONE THIS, BUT I'D LIKE TO MEET
IF YOU'D LIKE TO MEET ME,
HERE'S MY NUMBER

THAT'S THE END
SEND! SEND! SEND!

CURVY WIDOW'S LICKING HER LIPS
SHE'S SHAKING HER HIPS
LOOK OUT ALL YOU MEN
ACROSS THE WORLD WIDE WEB
CURVY WIDOW'S GOT YOU IN HER SITES!
THAT'S RIGHT

CURVY WIDOW'S GOT YOU IN HER SITES!

[MUSIC NO. 05A "CURVY STRUTS"]

(**BOBBY** *exits.*)

(Phone rings.)

(Voice-over.) Leave a message.

(Machine beeps.)

MORT. *(Voice-over.)* Is this Curvy Widow? I'm Mort. I just got your Match message. I'm a nice guy. Used to be in the clothing biz. I promise you I'm safe. How about a movie, and maybe dinner?

(Machine beeps.)

Scene Six: Pharmacy

(A counter. There is a prescription sign and rows of drugs with a large, very obvious condom display. **BOBBY** *enters with* **CAROLINE** *in tow. Both are in disguise.)*

BOBBY. *(To* **CAROLINE**.*)* When I was a teenager, only girls who chewed gum and went to drive-in movies used condoms. "Nice" girls had diaphragms.

CAROLINE. STDs are the new ABCs. Safe sex always, luv.

BOBBY. Thank god you're with me as my condom sherpa.

CAROLINE. I don't use them. I'm married. I'm just here in case you chicken out.

PHARMACIST. Can I help you? Are you dropping off a prescription?

BOBBY. *(Whispers.)* Where are the condoms?

(The **PHARMACIST** *doesn't hear her.)*

Where are the condoms?

(The **PHARMACIST** *still doesn't hear her.)*

CAROLINE. *(Loudly.)* Condoms!

PHARMACIST. Oh, condoms.

CAROLINE. Condoms.

PHARMACIST. They're right in front of you.

BOBBY & CAROLINE. Oh, my.

PHARMACIST. Colors, lubricated, ribbed, smooth, magnum.

BOBBY. Magnum? I thought that was a gun?

PHARMACIST. And flavored...

BOBBY & CAROLINE. Flavored?

(A **WOMAN** *who has been shopping on the periphery approaches* **BOBBY**.*)*

PRINCIE. Bobby? Bobby is that you? It's Princie – from Greenwich Country Day field hockey.

(**PRINCIE** *squeals with delight and runs to hug*
BOBBY. BOBBY *screams and grabs a box of*
condoms as she avoids the hug and exits with
CAROLINE.)

(Musical transition.)

Scene Seven: Bobby's Bedroom

[MUSIC NO. 05B "CONDOMS INTO DRESSING"]

(**BOBBY** *enters her apartment and starts primping and holding up different outfits.*)

BOBBY.
CURVY WIDOW'S GOT A DATE!
I CHOOSE A BLOUSE, LA, LA, LA, LA
WHAT THEN? WHAT THEN?

(**DEAD JIM** *enters.* **BOBBY** *screams. Music halts.*)

DEAD JIM. (*Grinning.*) Hi Bobby.

BOBBY. Jim!

DEAD JIM. It's me. In the flesh. Well I suppose that's an exaggeration.

BOBBY. You were cremated.

DEAD JIM. You put me in a can marked temporary.

BOBBY. You're on my "to-do" list.

DEAD JIM. I see you got rid of everything that was mine.

BOBBY. Ours Jim, ours.

DEADS JIM. Even my chair is gone?

BOBBY. Why are you back?

DEAD JIM. Why are you dating?

BOBBY. Look, I'm lonely. I was married my whole adult life and now I have to learn how to be single again. The last time I was on a date a shrimp cocktail cost a buck fifty.

DEAD JIM. You're my widow. Where is your respect? I haven't even been gone that long.

BOBBY. Don't you want me to be happy? To go on with my life?

DEAD JIM. Why would I?

BOBBY. Jim, you need to leave me alone.

DEAD JIM. Well I won't. And if you keep dating, you'll see me day and night.

BOBBY. Over my dead body.

DEAD JIM. Uh-uh. Over mine.

> *(Scene transition:* **MORT** *appears and finds his way into the movie theater.* **BOBBY** *crosses the stage and finds her way into...)*

[MUSIC NO. 05C "BUT DEATH DID US PART"]

Scene Eight: The Movie Theater

(BOBBY sits beside MORT and starts watching the screen. MORT and BOBBY share a popcorn and watch the movie. MORT begins to squirm, more and more.)

MORT. I'll be right back – I have prostate trouble.

(MORT squeezes past BOBBY toward the aisle.)

Do you need more popcorn?

BOBBY. No, I'll wait for the burger

MORT. You know we could skip the burger and just go to your place.

(BOBBY just stares at him, looking completely panicked. She gets up and runs out of the movie theater as MORT follows her.)

(Scene transition: BOBBY runs across the stage to land outside on the street.)

Slow down, slow down.

(BOBBY stops and tries to make herself small as MORT goes to embrace her. She shivers.)

Are you all right?

BOBBY. I'm fine.

(MORT tries to put her coat on her shoulders.)

No. Yes. No.

(Stops.)

Come upstairs.

(BOBBY leads MORT across the stage into her building entrance. The elevator door is opened by ELEVATOR MAN.)

ELEVATOR MAN. Good evening. Mrs. Goldman. Sir.

BOBBY. He's not Sir he's...

(Elevator music* plays as they all have an awkward ride up to Bobby's apartment. Bell rings and **ELEVATOR MAN** *opens the door, letting* **MORT** *and* **BOBBY** *out into her apartment.* **ELEVATOR MAN** *closes door and exits.)*

[MUSIC NO. 06 "A NEW HAND"]

MORT. *(Whistles.)* Nice place.

BOBBY. Uh-huh.

MORT.

    CAN I TOUCH YOU?

BOBBY.

    I DON'T KNOW YET

MORT.

    CAN I HOLD YOUR HAND?

BOBBY.

    YES... NO... SURE
    I'M SORRY. TRY AGAIN?

MORT.

    YOU LOOK LOVELY

BOBBY.

    YOU HAVE TO SAY THAT

MORT.

    CAN I KISS YOU?

BOBBY.

    YES... NO... OKAY GO

    (He tries to kiss her. She smacks him.)

    I'M SORRY
    ONE MORE TIME
    I WON'T HIT YOU

    IT'S A NEW HAND ON MY BACK

---

*A license to produce *Curvy Widow* does not include a performance license for any third-party or copyrighted music. Licensees should create an original composition or use music in the public domain. For further information, please see Music Use Note on page 3.

IT'S A NEW HAND ON MY ARM
THIS HAND OF A STRANGER
IT'S DIFFERENT AND DANGEROUS
WHAT DO I MAKE OF THIS HAND?
THIS NEW HAND

MORT.

MAY I UNDRESS YOU?

BOBBY.

IS THAT REQUIRED?

MORT.

I SORTA HAVE TO

BOBBY.

YES... NO...

> (**MORT** *tries to remove her blouse and she elbows him in the stomach.*)

OH.

MORT.

DON'T BE SORRY
I'LL GO SLOW
I WON'T HURT YOU

BOBBY.

IT'S A STRANGE TOUCH ON MY SKIN
SUCH A STRANGE TOUCH ON MY KNEE
THE MOMENT IS HERE
IT'S BEEN THIRTY-FIVE YEARS
IT JUST FEELS SO WEIRD

PLEASE GO

MORT.

YES? NO?

BOBBY.

...NO
I'M SORRY
YOU SHOULD STAY

> (**MORT** *begins to slowly, gently massage* **BOBBY**.)

BUT CAN YOU? OOO THAT FEELS NICE

IF YOU JUST – OOO THAT FEELS RIGHT
AND I'LL JUST – OOOO

I'D FORGOTTEN ABOUT NEW
I'D FORGOTTEN ABOUT FIRST TIMES
AND FOR THE FIRST TIME
IN A LONG TIME
I'M COMING TO LIFE
I'M COMING TO LIFE
AND IT'S OVER SO SOON

MORT.

CAN I HOLD YOU?

BOBBY.

IF YOU WANT TO
DON'T YOU NEED TO GO?

MORT.

YES... NO...

(She gives him a look that says "yes.")

YES
I'M SORRY

(He dresses quickly and exits.)

BOBBY.

NO IT'S FINE
TAKE YOUR TIME
DON'T BE SORRY
I'M NOT SORRY

THERE'S A NEW MAN OUT THE DOOR
A MAN I NEVER SAW BEFORE
HE WAS KIND AND POLITE
I GOT THROUGH THE NIGHT
AND THE WORLD DIDN'T END
AND THE SKY DIDN'T FALL
JUST NEW

THAT'S ALL

[MUSIC NO. 06A "NO SHRINKING VIOLET"]

(Scene transition: A good-looking **MAN** *crosses to center stage, looking through his phone and swiping. He sees a profile.)*

KEN. Curvy Widow. Sweet!

(He swipes right to "like" as he continues offstage.)

Scene Nine: Shrink's Office

(**SHRINK** *sits while* **BOBBY** *paces.*)

SHRINK. Will you sit down? You're making me dizzy.

BOBBY. Leave me alone. I've had a bad night.

SHRINK. Tell me about it.

BOBBY. I slept with a man.

SHRINK. Were you able to achieve orgasm?

BOBBY. What is this? Sex ed class?

(**BOBBY** *finally sits down.*)

Yes, everything worked.

(*Hangs head.*)

But the minute he left – guilt, guilt, guilt, and more guilt.

SHRINK. Can't you be a widow and still want to be with a man?

BOBBY. (*Shrug.*) I suppose so. It's just that I should be a *grieving* widow but now I'm a piece of ass.

SHRINK. (*Grins.*) Is that so bad? You're a vital, interesting, attractive woman.

BOBBY. Knock it off.

SHRINK. Bobby, I think you should continue dating. It's really good for you.

BOBBY. Do you send all your widow clients into slutdom?

(*Musical transition.*)

Scene Ten: Various Dates

*(Bobby's three **FRIENDS** enter across the stage.)*

[MUSIC NO. 07 "IT'S NOT A MATCH"]

BOBBY.

ONCE THE SEAL GETS BROKEN.
IT'S VERY HARD TO STOP
PANDORA'S BOX GETS OPENED
AND THE CHERRY'S POPPED

I THOUGHT ONE DATE MIGHT
FILL THE GAP
INSTEAD THE GAP'S BECOMING
A VENUS FLYTRAP!

HEIDI.

TO FIND A DATE YOU DON'T HATE
YOU FIND A SITE FOR MATES

CAROLINE & JOAN.

THEN YOU WAIT AND WAIT
WHILE THEY SERVE YOU UP LIKE BAIT

JOAN.

THEN WHEN SOMEBODY BITES
YOUR SENSE OF SELF-WORTH INFLATES

HEIDI.

IT'S THE MARCH OF DATES

> *(**BOBBY**'s date with **STAN**. They're in the lobby of a museum. **STAN**'s shirt is unbuttoned to the waist, with a huge stomach like he swallowed a basketball, covered with a thick mat of hair.)*

STAN.

YOU MUST BE BOBBY. I'M STAN
HERE – PUT ON THIS PIN
SO WE CAN GET IN THE MUSEUM

I'VE PAID YOUR ENTRANCE FEE
THAT'S, UH, THIRTEEN DOLLARS YOU OWE ME

FEMALE ENSEMBLE.

> IT'S NOT A MATCH
> IT'S NOT A MATCH
> HE ISN'T WORTH A SECOND LOOK
> OR SECOND CHANCE
> SO TAKE A PASS
> IT'S NOT A MATCH
> HE IS A MISERABLE CATCH SO THROW HIM BACK

BOBBY.

> I FOUND THE EXIT AND I FLED
> AND ON THE STEPS I CLEAR MY HEAD
> WHEN YOU DATE, YOU GET BURNED
> BUT LESSON LEARNED:
> IT'S A NEW WORLD BUT I'M STILL OLD-FASHIONED
> MEN NEED TO SHOW THEY CAN SPEND
>
> BUT ONCE THE WHEEL'S IN MOTION
> IT'S HARD TO HIT REVERSE
> EVEN WHEN YOUR DATES GO FROM
> BAD TO WORSE

> > *(Switch dates to* **GUY**. *He is in a three-piece suit and wearing a really bad toupee.* **GUY** *and* **BOBBY** *are mid-argument.)*

GUY.

> I'M SORRY TO SEE
> THAT YOU'RE OLDER THAN YOU SHOULD BE
> BY A FACTOR OF THREE

BOBBY. What? I don't understand.

GUY.

> THERE'S A FORMULA
> DETERMINING DESIRABLE AGE
> A WOMAN SHOULD BE ONE HALF THE MAN'S AGE
> PLUS SEVEN

BOBBY.

> THAT'S RIDICULOUS AND ASININE
> THAT WOULD MEAN THE MAN FOR ME IS NINETY-NINE!

FEMALE ENSEMBLE.

> IT'S NOT A MATCH

IT'S NOT A MATCH
HE ISN'T WORTH A SECOND LOOK
OR SECOND CHANCE
SO TAKE A PASS
IT'S NOT A MATCH
HE IS A MISERABLE CATCH SO THROW HIM BACK

BOBBY.

I GAVE HIM HELL AND THEN I RAN
AND ALL AT ONCE I UNDERSTAND
WHEN YOU DATE, YOU GET BURNED
BUT LESSON LEARNED:
SOME MEN ARE ONLY OUT HUNTING
THEY DON'T REALLY LIKE WOMEN AT ALL

CAROLINE.

TO HAVE A GREAT FIRST DATE
LET HIM CHOOSE THE TIME AND PLACE

HEIDI.

LET HIM SET THE PACE

JOAN.

SO YOU CAN QUICKLY JUDGE HIS TASTE

CAROLINE.

IF HE'S AWFUL YOU LEAVE

CAROLINE, JOAN & HEIDI.

YOU DON'T HAVE THE WHOLE NIGHT TO WASTE

JOAN.

ON THE MARCH OF DATES

> (**BOBBY** *and* **PETER** *are exiting a restaurant,*
> *laughing and enjoying each other's company.)*

BOBBY. That was a terrific first date.

PETER. *(Suddenly.)* It's over.

BOBBY. But we have so much in common.

PETER.

IT'S TRUE WE DO
AND I'VE LOVED
I MEAN I'VE LOVED TALKING WITH YOU
I'VE ENJOYED THE WINE
I'VE ENJOYED THE DUCK

THAT WE MET EACH OTHER IS A STROKE OF LUCK
BUT YOU'RE FAR TOO SMART
TO BE SOMEONE THAT I F–

BOBBY. Forget it!

FEMALE ENSEMBLE.

IT'S NOT A MATCH
IT'S NOT A –

BOBBY. *(Interrupting.)* Okay, okay.

I GO BACK HOME AND POUR A DRINK
AND ON THE COUCH I START TO THINK
WHEN YOU DATE YOU GET BURNED
BUT LESSON LEARNED:
SINGLE MEN MY AGE ARE AWFUL
THERE'S A REASON THAT THEY ARE ALONE

TO FIND A BETTER DATE
THERE'S GOT TO BE A BETTER WAY

ENSEMBLE.

IT'S NOT A MATCH!

Scene Eleven: Bobby's Bedroom – Christmas Eve

(There is a small, pathetic tree and computer screen. **BOBBY** *is barely tending to the tree.)*

CAROLINE, JOAN & HEIDI.
WE WISH YOU A MERRY CHRISTMAS
WE WISH YOU A MERRY CHRISTMAS
WE WISH YOU A MERRY CHRISTMAS
AND A HAPPY NEW YEAR

WE WON'T GO UNTIL WE GET SOME
WE WON'T GO UNTIL WE GET SOME
WE WON'T GO UNTIL WE GET SOME

BOBBY. *(Interrupting.)* Go! Go!

*(**CAROLINE** and **HEIDI** scurry offstage.)*

JOAN. *(Slowly exiting.)* Well, I'm going to go get some.

*(**DEAD JIM** enters.)*

DEAD JIM. No lights? No tinsel? No garland?

BOBBY. Maybe you could just say Merry Christmas.

DEAD JIM. I see that you have had no luck dating.

BOBBY. I've had plenty of luck. Just none of it good.

DEAD JIM. Why won't you admit it? Widows are old and grey and come with their own mahjong boards.

BOBBY. Be gone ghost of Christmas past!!

DEAD JIM. *(A cappella.)*
I'M NOT GONNA LET YOU GET SOME
I'M NOT GONNA LET YOU GET SOME

(Humming as he exits.)

(Finally alone, **BOBBY** *sits on the bed, completely depressed.)*

BOBBY. *(To herself.)* Forget Match.com. Let's see what's out there.

(She types.)

Adult. Dating. Sites.

(She clicks.)

BOBBY. This looks like fun. Promises adult companionship. Trial membership is free. I love free. Fill out profile. Okay. Post a photo. That's a big no. Join and search.

(Pause.)

[MUSIC NO. 08 "CURVY WIDOW – REPRISE"]

OH MY GOD OH MY GOD
WHAT IS THIS SITE?
EVERYONE NAKED IN TERRIBLE LIGHT
THIS MUST BE A SEX SITE
BOBBY GOLDMAN
JOINED A SEX SITE

(**BOBBY** *starts to pace near the computer.*)

I should just delete my profile and close the account before my email address finds its way to the Russian mob.

(Shudders.)

What kind of desperate people would use this site? What is that woman wearing?

(Shakes her head.)

I'm being ridiculous. And judgmental. Maybe I should give it a shot.

CURVY WIDOW'S NOT ASHAMED
CURVY WIDOW'S NOT AFRAID
NO
SHE WANTS WHAT SHE WANTS

AND SHE GETS WHAT SHE WANTS
'CAUSE SHE TAKES WHAT SHE WANTS
AND SHE WANTS TO GET...

Oh boy.

CURVY WIDOW'S LICKING HER LIPS
SHE'S SHAKING...
SHE'S SHAKING...

WHO HAVE I BECOME?
SOMEONE INTERESTING
SOMEONE WHO'S NOT AFRAID

TO TRY NEW THINGS
I ALREADY FELL IN THE DEEP END
TIME TO SWIM, SWIM, SWIM, SWIM

>(**BOBBY** *clicks.*)

Submit.

>(*She screams.*)

AHHHHHHHHHHH
Oh my god! What have I done?

>(**BOBBY** *exits as the stage is flooded with* **PEOPLE** *trolling the internet.*)

[MUSIC NO. 08A "LOG ON, GET OFF"]

ENSEMBLE.

SEEKING COMPANIONS, BUT FEELING EXTREME?
WANTING CONNECTION, YOU KNOW WHAT I MEAN?
A LITTLE SUBVERSIVE, A LITTLE OBSCENE?
LOG ON, GET OFF

CRAVING DISTRACTION, I THROW YOU A LINE
BUILDING ATTRACTION, YOU SEND ME A SIGN

MALE ENSEMBLE.

THEN SOMEONE TAKES ACTION:

FEMALE ENSEMBLE.

YOUR PLACE OR MINE?

ENSEMBLE.

LOG ON, GET OFF

SURFING THROUGH A STRANGE LAND
REACHING OUT TO STRANGERS
A SEXY SECRET PLAYLAND
LET'S RENDEZVOUS
RIGHT NOW WILL DO

JUST MAKE A WISH AND PUT IT ON DISPLAY
IF YOU PERSIST THEN IT MIGHT BE YOUR DAY

TRY TO RESIST BUT YOU CAN'T KEEP AWAY

LOG ON, LOG ON, LOG ON, LOG ON, LOG ON
GET OFF

    (The **ENSEMBLE** *exits as* **BOBBY** *re-enters.)*

Scene Twelve: Bobby's Bedroom

(**BOBBY** *is nervously pacing around her computer.*)

BOBBY. *(To computer.)* Stop staring at me. It's only been an hour and a half. Why on earth am I scared? Take the rejection and then go watch another rerun of *Law and Order*.

(*She opens her laptop and hits a bunch of buttons. A musical flourish.*)

Oh my god!

[MUSIC NO. 09 "THE RULES FOR WHITTLING DOWN"]

ONE HUNDRED AND FIFTY-THREE
MEN WHO MAYBE WANT TO SLEEP WITH ME
ONE HUNDRED AND FIFTY-THREE
FROM A SEX SITE ON CHRISTMAS EVE
ONE HUNDRED AND FIFTY-THREE
DON'T EVEN NEED TO SEE A PIC OF ME
SHOULD I BE FLATTERED OR APPALLED?

I'VE GOT TO WHITTLE IT DOWN, WHITTLE IT DOWN,
WHITTLE IT DOWN
THERE HAS GOT TO BE A SYSTEMATIC
WAY IN WHICH TO NARROW DOWN
THE QUEUE OF MEN
INSIDE MY BOX

My inbox.

The Rules For Whittling Down.

CAN WE ADDRESS THE DICK PICS?

(*The* **ENSEMBLE MEN** *enter.*)

SO MANY DICK PICS
THOUGHTFULLY PLACED NEXT TO HOUSEHOLD
OBJECTS FOR REFERENCE

(*The* **ENSEMBLE MEN** *hold up the various mentioned items.*)

BOBBY.

REMOTES, BEER CANS, EGGPLANTS
YES LET'S DELETE THE DICK PICS

(*The* **ENSEMBLE MEN** *exit dejectedly.*)

NOW WE'RE DOWN TO SEVENTY-TWO
MEN WHO MAYBE I'D WANNA DO
NOW WE'RE DOWN TO SEVENTY-TWO
MEN WHO MAYBE WANNA DO ME TOO
NOW WE'RE DOWN TO SEVENTY-TWO
TOO MANY TO WRITE BACK TO
I NEED ANOTHER ROUND OF CUTS

I'VE GOT TO WHITTLE IT DOWN, WHITTLE IT DOWN,
WHITTLE IT DOWN
JUST A LITTLE TASK TO PROJECT MANAGE
ORGANIZE AND SORT AND CULL
THE STEADY STREAM
OF HORNY MEN

The Rules For Whittling Down, Continued.

LET'S TALK ABOUT THE HEADLINES

(*The* **ENSEMBLE MEN** *re-enter variously.*)

DISGUSTING HEADLINES
SPLATTERED ACROSS THESE PROSPECTS'
PROFILES IN PUBLIC
"I LIKE TO LICK,"

(**FIRST ENSEMBLE MAN** *demonstrates.*)

"EAT YOUR FEET,"

(**SECOND ENSEMBLE MAN** *demonstrates.*)

"PUT ME IN YOU"

(**LAST ENSEMBLE MAN** *demonstrates.*)

YES, LET'S DELETE GROSS HEADLINES

(*The* **ENSEMBLE MEN** *enter triumphantly.*)

WHO'S THE ONE TO CHOOSE?
LET'S READ FOR CLUES

Dear Curvy Widow – I believe the man is the boss – is
that a problem?

DELETE!

Dear Curvy Widow, send pic you sound old –

DELETE!

Dear Curvy *Window* –

DELETE!

Dear Curvy Widow, you sound terrific. Hope we can meet. With kisses, Kevin, Barry and Gladys –

DELETE DELETE DELETE!

   NOW I'M ONLY LEFT WITH NINE
   POTENTIAL PARTNERS FOR SEXY TIME
   NOW I'M ONLY LEFT WITH NINE
   WE'RE COMING DOWN TO CHOOSING TIME
   NOW I'M ONLY LEFT WITH NINE
   AND THE CHOICE IS MINE ALL MINE
   IT'S TIME TO PICK MY POISON –

     (Music stops as a very distinguished gentleman
     enters.)

MARSHALL. Dear Curvy, I'm a retired businessman and a widower. I live on Central Park South, here is my cell number. I'd be honored if you would give me a call.

BOBBY.

   GRAMMAR IS GOOD, PICTURE IS FINE
   STRONG BUT POLITE, THE BEST OF THE NINE
   BUSINESSMAN, CENTRAL PARK SOUTH, WIDOWER
   ALL GOOD SIGNS

     (MARSHALL *exits.)*

   I'VE SUCCESSFULLY TRASHED
   ALL THE PIGS AND PATHETICS AND FOOLS
   APPLYING THE RULES FOR WHITTLING DOWN
   JUST A LITTLE WHITTLING DOWN

Scene Thirteen: Bar at Essex House / Central Park South Bedroom

[MUSIC NO. 09A "DRYNESS MAY OCCUR"]

(There is a back bar. **BOBBY** *enters and is waved over to the bar by an attractive man, her date,* **MARSHALL**.*)*

MARSHALL. Bobby, I would know you anywhere. I'm Marshall.

BOBBY. Hi, Merry Christmas.

(She smiles as he gives her a kiss on the cheek and a small hug.)

MARSHALL. I'm so glad you agreed to meet. What can I get you to drink?

*(***MARSHALL*** crosses to bar as ***BOBBY*** turns toward the audience.)*

BOBBY. Well this is different. After sixty-five dates on Match no one except the man who took my widow maidenhead had even smiled at me.

*(***BOBBY*** smiles at her date.)*

(To **MARSHALL**.*)* Campari and soda please, with two orange slices.

(Underscoring and set indicate time passing. **BOBBY** *and* **MARSHALL** *are huddled together. They are smiling, touching, and talking animatedly. It's obvious that they are having a wonderful time getting to know each other.)*

BARTENDER. Last call, please, ladies and gentlemen.

MARSHALL. Look, you're terrific and I don't want this to end. Could I entice you to come back to my place?

BOBBY. I just met you.

MARSHALL. Wouldn't it be nice to be with another person? Don't you ever feel lonely?

(Underscoring stops.)

BOBBY. *(To audience.)* One: I'm freaked being propositioned on Christmas Eve from a man I just met on a sex site. Two: But look at him – what a holiday treat. Jingle bells!

MARSHALL. Bobby?

BOBBY. Wait a sec... I'm still weighing the pros and cons. Done.

　　　(Shift to: Central Park South bedroom.)

　　　*(**MARSHALL** kisses her then passionately walks her to bedroom offstage. The music swells until...)*

MARSHALL. *(Offstage.)* Are you ready?

BOBBY. *(Offstage.)* Yes, yes, yes...

　　　(Screams – Offstage/running on.)

No, nope, nope, nope, nope, nope, nope!

　　　(They run back onstage.)

I'm really sorry. That's never happened before. I don't know why it hurts so much.

MARSHALL. Oh you're frigid. This is your fault.

BOBBY. What?

MARSHALL. Look, I bought you drinks. I gave you tons of foreplay. I did my job. I think you need to leave.

　　　*(**MARSHALL** exits.)*

BOBBY. *(To audience.)* Merry Christmas to me; talk about getting a lump of coal. He's a certifiable dick. But what is happening to my body? Why on earth have I closed as tight as... I'm at a loss for a suitable metaphor.

[MUSIC NO. 10 "THE GYNECOLOGIST TANGO"]

A VISIT TO THE GYNECOLOGIST
TO FIND OUT WHAT ON EARTH'S
THE MATTER WITH ME
WHY WHEN I FINALLY FOUND
A SOURCE OF GOOD MEN

DOES IT HURT SO MUCH
IT MAKES ME WANT TO
NEVER EVER LET SOMEONE TOUCH ME AGAIN!

(**DR. GILBERT** *and his* **NURSE** *enter.*)

DR. GILBERT PLEASE TELL ME WHAT TO DO

DR. GILBERT.

IT'S CLEAR TO ME WHAT'S HAPPENING
THE PROBLEM I'VE DEDUCED
A WOMAN OF YOUR AGE
HAS HORMONE LEVELS QUITE REDUCED
WHICH LEADS TO LUBRICATION LACK
AND CHANGES IN ACIDITY
DRYNESS, PAINFUL INTERCOURSE
AND LOSS OF ELASTICITY

BOBBY.

THANK GOD YOU HAVE THE ANSWERS DOC
SO TELL ME HOW TO FIX IT

DR. GILBERT.

THERE'S TREATMENTS, YES, BUT AT YOUR AGE
I DON'T THINK YOU SHOULD RISK IT
REPLACING HORMONES BRINGS A CHANCE
OF HARMFUL SIDE EFFECTS
AND IT ISN'T THAT IMPORTANT
SINCE IT ONLY HURTS WITH SEX

BOBBY. Only with sex?? Doctors throw Viagra at men like
confetti. Why shouldn't women want to have sex?

NURSE. All the time!

(**NURSE** *high-fives* **BOBBY. DR. GILBERT** *and his*
NURSE *exit as* **CAROLINE** *enters from the other
side of the stage.*)

CAROLINE.

I HAVE ANOTHER GYNECOLOGIST
THE ONE WHO HELPED ME THROUGH
MY CRISIS LAST YEAR
HE'S GOT THE SOLUTION
I PROMISE HE DOES
JUST TRUST WHAT HE SAYS

AND DO WHAT HE ASKS
IF YOU EVER WANT TO LET SOMEONE
TOUCH YOU AGAIN

    *(**DR. RODGERS** enters.)*

BOBBY & CAROLINE.

DR. RODGERS PLEASE TELL ME/HER WHAT TO DO

    *(**CAROLINE** exits.)*

DR. RODGERS.

REPLACING YOUR LOST HORMONES
CAN BE DONE BIOIDENTICALLY
AND WE MINIMIZE THE DANGER
BY NOT TREATING YOU SYSTEMICALLY
I'M PRESCRIBING YOU A HORMONE RING
TO KEEP THE PAIN AT BAY
INSERT IT WHEN YOU GET HOME
AND CHANGE IT EVERY NINETY DAYS

    *(**DR. RODGERS** exits.)*

BOBBY. That seems easy enough. Let me just get this open – It's the size of a plate! Am I supposed to bend it in half to insert it?

    *(**BOBBY** bends it in half and it flies out of her reach. She goes after it, bends it again, and it flies across the room. She picks it up again and tosses it into the audience.)*

Here, you try it.

    *(Bobby's three **FRIENDS** enter the stage.)*

I TRY SO MANY GYNECOLOGISTS
AND EVERY G-Y-N JUST TELLS ME AGAIN

FEMALES.

IT'S PART OF GETTING OLDER
IT'S NATURAL WITH AGE

BOBBY.

BUT I JUST CAN'T ACCEPT IT
THERE MUST BE A WAY
I'M NOT CLOSING SHOP

AND JUST WALKING AWAY
I'M STILL YOUNG AT HEART
AND I'M STARTING MY SEX LIFE ANEW

WON'T SOMEONE TELL ME WHAT TO DO?

HEIDI.
I COULD GIVE YOU A PINT OF ICE CREAM
I COULD GIVE YOU MY SYMPATHY
I COULD GIVE YOU A HUG
BUT I WON'T
AND INSTEAD
I GIVE YOU
MY HERO DR. DOUG

FEMALES.
DR. DOUG

> (**DR. DOUG** *enters from the wings with samples in his hand. He clasps his arms together over his head like a winner athlete.*)

DR. DOUG. Easy fix!
HAVING SEX IS FUN – EVEN OVER FIFTY-FIVE
IT'S WHAT KEEPS YOU YOUNG
AND MAKES YOU FEEL ALIVE
THIS TEENY TINY PILL
CONTAINS A SAFE AND TESTED DRUG
INSERT IT ONCE A WEEK
YOU'LL START TO FEEL THE CHANGE
THEN USE IT LESS
YOU'LL KNOW WHAT'S RIGHT
TRUST YOURSELF
TRUST YOUR BODY
IN A MONTH YOU WILL BE THANKING ME
OR MY NAME'S NOT DR. DOUG

FEMALES.
DR. DOUG!

BOBBY. What is it? A fuel additive?

DR. DOUG. Close. It's called VagiFem.

> (**DR. DOUG** *exits.*)

BOBBY.
> VAGIFEM
> THAT'S RIGHT – VAGIFEM
> THANKS TO VAGIFEM, MY G-Y-N
> GOT ME

BOBBY & FEMALES.
> BACK ON MY BACK AGAIN

[MUSIC NO. 10A "TANGO AWAY"]

Scene Fourteen: Bobby's Bedroom

(**DEAD JIM** *walks in.*)

DEAD JIM. More men? You are Mrs. James Goldman. You are becoming tabloid fodder. My friends are cringing. You're embarrassing me.

BOBBY. Embarrassing you? How do you think I feel? I'm trying to piece a life together.

DEAD JIM. And you think you're going to find it sleeping with men off of sex sites?

BOBBY. I've tried most everything else so unless you have a better suggestion that's exactly what I am going to do.

DEAD JIM. Did I make you happy?

BOBBY. I think so.

DEAD JIM. You're not sure? You know I tried.

BOBBY. *(She smiles.)* I know you did.

DEAD JIM. Great. Then you'll stop dating other men?

BOBBY. Under the circumstances, that's an unreasonable request.

DEAD JIM. Unreasonable? And this surprises you?

(**DEAD JIM** *exits.* **BOBBY** *preps to go out.*)

BOBBY. Just you wait. I'll show you unreasonable.

(Scene transition: **BOBBY** *primps herself as the* **ENSEMBLE** *transforms the stage with the following song.)*

[MUSIC NO. 11 "THE DOCTOR DELIVERS"]

CURVY WIDOW'S LICKING HER LIPS
SHE'S SHAKING HER HIPS
LOOK OUT ALL YOU MEN
ACROSS THE WORLD WIDE WEB

Scene Fourteen: Upscale East Side Restaurant

> (**BOBBY** *is seated with an attractive* **MAN**. *Everything looks like it's going well.* **HEIDI** *is seated at the bar where* **BOBBY** *can't see her. She glances at* **BOBBY**'s *table occasionally.*)

> (*A* **WAITRESS** *approaches* **BOBBY** *and* **SIMON** *and starts to ask if they want coffee and dessert.*)

SIMON. (*Looks at his watch.*) You don't want dessert, do you?

BOBBY. Well. I was enjoying the even–

SIMON. (*Interrupting.*) You go ahead. I need to go. My dog has been alone for too long.

> (*He takes a couple of bills from his wallet and puts them on the table.*)

If it's a bit more for the check you'll cover it, okay?

> (**SIMON** *gets up and exits past* **HEIDI**.)

BOBBY. Of all the insane, lousy...

HEIDI. (*To* **SIMON**.) *You're* the dog!!

BOBBY. Heidi? What on earth...?

HEIDI. (*Interrupting* **BOBBY**.) I didn't like the sound of that guy when you told us about him. Figured you could use a wingman.

> (**HEIDI** *crosses to* **BOBBY**'s *table.*)

BOBBY. I just don't understand! Just as Dr. Doug works his miracles, now all my dates suck.

HEIDI. I'm convinced that most men were raised by wolves. Except for Charlie. I never realized how wonderful my husband is until now.

BOBBY. Oh sure. Talk about how wonderful your husband is when a man just left me for his dog.

HEIDI. Fair point. I just wish all the good ones weren't married.

BOBBY. I know.

> *(Bell tone.)*

I know.

> (**BOBBY** *and* **HEIDI** *exit as three very attractive* **BUSINESSMEN** *enter.)*

[MUSIC NO. 12 "LOOKING FOR"]

MARRIED MAN 1.

I AM LOOKING FOR...

MARRIED MAN 2.

I AM LOOKING FOR...

MARRIED MAN 3.

I AM LOOKING FOR...

ALL THREE.

A SMART SOPHISTICATED ELEGANT WOMAN

MARRIED MAN 2.

A WOMAN WHO ENJOYS A NICE ROMANTIC DINNER

MARRIED MAN 3.

YES A

ALL THREE.

SMART SOPHISTICATED ELEGANT WOMAN

MARRIED MAN 1.

TO FIT SEAMLESSLY INTO MY LIFE

ALL THREE.

A WOMAN WHO ISN'T MY WIFE
IT'S NOT WHAT YOU THINK

MARRIED MAN 3.

WE GO TO MOVIES

ALL THREE.

IT'S NOT WHAT YOU THINK

MARRIED MAN 2.

WE CAN DISCUSS OUR BUS'NESSES

ALL THREE.

NO THIS IS NOT A MISTRESS

MARRIED MAN 1 & 2.

OR A PIECE ON THE SIDE

MARRIED MAN 2.

> I CAN TAKE HER OUT IN PUBLIC
> AND WE DON'T HAVE TO HIDE

MARRIED MAN 1.

> SHE CAN KEEP UP CONVERSATION
> LIKE SHE SITS ON MY BOARD

ALL THREE.

> THAT'S THE REASON WHY
> I'M HAPPY TO EXPLORE

MARRIED MAN 1.

> LOOKING FOR...

MARRIED MAN 2.

> LOOKING FOR...

MARRIED MAN 3.

> LOOKING FOR...

MARRIED MAN 1.

> I'M A CEO WHO'S ALWAYS ON THE ROAD.

MARRIED MAN 2.

> I'M A SURGEON

MARRIED MAN 3.

> A STATE SENATOR.

ALL THREE.

> WE'RE ALL VERY BUSY.

MARRIED MAN 1.

> BUT IF I CAN FIND A WAY TO SPEND AN EVENING

MARRIED MAN 3.

> AND I MAY ENJOY A MEAL

MARRIED MAN 1.

> AT SOMEPLACE NICE

MARRIED MAN 2.

> AND GET A LAUGH

MARRIED MAN 3.

> OR GET ADVICE

ALL THREE.

> FROM SUCH A SMART, SOPHISTICATED
> ELEGANT WOMAN
> WHO RESPECTS THE COMPLICATIONS OF MY LIFE

MARRIED MAN 1.

WELL THEN WHERE'S THE HARM?

MARRIED MAN 2.

REALLY, WHERE'S THE HARM?

MARRIED MAN 3.

I MEAN WHERE'S THE HARM?

ALL THREE.

BUT STILL AND ALL OF COURSE

DON'T TELL MY WIFE

IT'S NOT WHAT YOU THINK

MARRIED MAN 3.

SHE PAYS ATTENTION

ALL THREE.

IT'S NOT WHAT YOU THINK

MARRIED MAN 1.

WE HAVE A REAL CONNECTION

ALL THREE.

IT'S AN EXCELLENT ARRANGEMENT

THOUGH I GET THAT IT'S STRANGE

I'VE A COMFORTABLE DOMESTIC LIFE

I DON'T WANT TO CHANGE

THERE'S NO DANGER TO MY MARRIAGE

THAT WOULD MERIT CONCERN

THAT'S THE REASON I CONTINUE TO RETURN...

MARRIED MAN 1.

TO RETURN...

ALL THREE.

TO THIS SMART, SOPHISTICATED ELEGANT WOMAN

MARRIED MAN 1.

CALLED CURVY

MARRIED MAN 2.

YES, CURVY

MARRIED MAN 3.

AH, CURVY

MARRIED MAN 1.

SHE'S LIKE A LONG WALK TO DE-STRESS ME

MARRIED MAN 2.

LIKE A DAY SPA TO REFRESH ME

MARRIED MAN 3.

LIKE A FINE WINE SHE DELIGHTS ME

MARRIED MAN 1.

LIKE A SPORTS CAR SHE EXCITES ME

ALL THREE.

IT'S NOT WHAT YOU THINK

WE'VE ALL GOT OUR SECRETS

IT MAY SEEM COMPLEX

BUT IT'S NOT ABOUT SEX

IT'S A RELATIONSHIP

PART OF MY HAPPILY MARRIED LIFE

(PLEASE DON'T TELL MY WIFE)

Scene Fifteen: Bar

[MUSIC NO. 12A "RESTAURANT INCIDENTAL"]

*(**JOAN** is at a table near the bar of an upscale watering hole. **BOBBY** has stepped away to take a phone call.)*

BOBBY. *(On cell.)* Perfect babe. I'll meet you at eight. Can't wait.

(Listening to phone.)

You're delicious.

(Hangs up.)

JOAN. *(To **BOBBY**, admiringly.)* You're smooth, very smooth. That's the second guy who's called you since we've been here.

(Looking around at the men at the bar.)

BOBBY. I don't know how it happened.

JOAN. Look, count your blessings. Don't look a gift horse in the mouth. A bird in the hand is worth two in the –

BOBBY. Don't say it.

(Beat.)

I was so worried about competing with the "under forty" set. Yet here I am: awash in male companionship.

JOAN. Storming the beaches. Taking no prisoners. You've become the Navy SEAL of dating.

BOBBY. I like that.

JOAN. Bobby, you know I would rather slit my wrists than get all mushy with you.

BOBBY. That's why I respect you.

JOAN. You built your new loft, you stopped dressing like your mother and you are dating prime beefcake. You're not screwing up your life.

BOBBY. If that were a compliment I'd thank you.

JOAN. Well it's not. So don't.

(**BOBBY** *grins.*)

Now I should really get going.

(**JOAN** *starts to ask for the bill. An* **ATTRACTIVE MAN** *enters and sits at the bar near them.*)

BOBBY. I'll get this.

JOAN. (*Laughs as she exits.*) Call you tomorrow luv.

(**BOBBY** *finishes her drink and starts to rummage in her bag for her wallet.*)

ATTRACTIVE MAN (PER SE). (*Coming over to her table.*) Please, let me.

BOBBY. Thank you but I have this.

PER SE. I guess I'm rusty. I didn't mean to offend you. I'm just stopping off for a nightcap before I take the train home to Chappaqua.

BOBBY. It's a lovely area. I've worked there on projects for many years.

PER SE. Projects?

BOBBY. Yes. I own a construction company.

PER SE. That's very enticing. You certainly don't see many women in that field.

(**PER SE** *hands* **BOBBY** *his card.*)

Here, I didn't want you to think I was just some gigolo preying on a beautiful woman.

(*She laughs, looks at card.*)

BOBBY. CEO of a heavy machinery manufacturing company. You may have picked up the only woman in New York who owns marble saws.

PER SE. What size marble saws?

BOBBY. You certainly know how to sweet talk.

PER SE. It's in the company manual. How long have you been in construction?

BOBBY. Thirty-six years. Unlisted company for very specific clientele.

PER SE. I'm impressed.

BOBBY. No need to be. Now, I'm truly enjoying you but I'm actually meeting someone.

[MUSIC NO. 12B "YOU SEEM INTERESTING"]

FEMALE PATRON.

WHOEVER YOU ARE YOU SEEM INTERESTING

PER SE. I'm traveling next week but when I'm back, have dinner with me at Per Se?

COCKTAIL WAITRESS.

TWO TOTAL STRANGERS...

MALE PATRON.

...BUT NOT FOR LONG

BOBBY. *(As she exits.)* I'd like that.

BARTENDER.

A WINK AND A LAUGH

(**BOBBY** *smiles and gives him her card.)*

FEMALE PATRON.

AND A NUMBER

ALL.

SO IT STARTS

Scene Sixteen: Outside Gramercy Tavern

DATE. You usually love Gramercy Tavern. Are you okay?

BOBBY. Of course. Fine.

DATE. Not only did you not eat your shrimp, you didn't finish my dessert.

BOBBY. Well, my tummy is not quite...

DATE. I'm sending you home.

> (**BOBBY** *starts to object.*)

You need to get home, period. Taxi!

BOBBY. Okay. But I'm sure I'm fine.

> (*He walks her toward the curb and shakes her hand goodbye.*)

You're shaking my hand? I just have a little indigestion.

DATE. (*Exiting.*) I can't take the chance of catching anything – I'm married. But I will call you tomorrow.

BOBBY. I'm not Typhoid Mary!!

> (**BOBBY**'s *stomach starts to cramp. She rounds the periphery of the stage as quickly as possible to arrive at...*)
>
> (*Scene: Bobby's bathroom.*)
>
> (**BOBBY** *is propped up on the floor next to the toilet, moaning with stomach flu pains.*)

[MUSIC NO. 13 "LYING ON THE BATHROOM FLOOR"]

WELL AREN'T I A PRETTY SIGHT?
LYING ON THE BATHROOM FLOOR
I FEEL EVER SO ELEGANT
A PROPER PRINCESS
ON HER THRONE

> (*Laughs painfully.*)

(GROAN)

I THINK I'M GIVING UP THE FIGHT
I'M STAYING PUT HERE ON THE BATHROOM FLOOR

WHO KNEW IT WAS POSSIBLE
TO REGURGITATE
MORE THAN I ATE

I WISH SOMEONE COULD BRING ME A WASHCLOTH
A GINGER ALE
PEPTO BISMOL
OR A PISTOL
I MISS HIM

> *(She gives in and lies fully down on the floor.)*

I GUESS EVERYTHING'S ALL RIGHT
IT'S KIND OF NICE HERE ON THE BATHROOM FLOOR
THESE COLD TILES AGAINST MY SKIN
FEELS LIKE A WIN

> *(She pulls herself back up.)*

STILL IT'D BE NICE TO FIND A GUY
TO HELP ME UP OFF OF THE BATHROOM FLOOR
SOMEONE WHO'LL STAY THE NIGHT
OR MORE

> *(***BOBBY*** *exits.)*

> *(Scene: Bare stage.)*

> *(Three* **MEN** *walk onstage.* **FIRST MAN** *answers his phone.)*

[MUSIC NO. 14 "LOOKING FOR - REPRISE"]

MARRIED MAN 1.

I AM LOOKING FOR...
Curvy, you know I can't see you on weekends and holidays.

> *(***SECOND MAN*** *answers his phone.)*

MARRIED MAN 2.

I AM LOOKING FOR...
I thought you understood my situation.

> *(***THIRD MAN*** *answers his phone.)*

MARRIED MAN 3.

I AM LOOKING FOR...

What do you mean I don't understand?

ALL THREE.

MY SMART, SOPHISTICATED, ELEGANT WOMAN

MARRIED MAN 3. Goodbye?

ALL THREE.

GOODBYE

PLEASE DON'T TELL MY WIFE

> *(Scene transition: All of the* **MEN** *exit as* **BOBBY** *browses the fruit section of the grocery store.)*

Scene Eighteen: Fancy Food Store

(**BOBBY** *is food shopping and* **PER SE** *enters. They cross each other before he recognizes her.*)

PER SE. Bobby. Hey there.

BOBBY. Oh. Hi.

PER SE. How are the marble saws?

BOBBY. Very happy and very busy.

PER SE. (*Looking at her basket.*) Someone is getting a beautiful dinner.

BOBBY. Well. Just a few friends coming over. How's Chappaqua?

PER SE. In the suburbs. You never called me back.

BOBBY. I wanted to. Really. But I decided to stop going out with mar...

PER SE. I'm separated.

BOBBY. Prove it.

(**PER SE** *shows* **BOBBY** *his shopping basket and reveals a Hungry Man frozen dinner.*)

So. Per Se, next Thursday?

(*They look at each other and exit on opposite sides of the stage.*)

(*Scene: Fitness studio*)

[MUSIC NO. 15 "THE ONE"]

(*We see* **CAROLINE** *and* **HEIDI** *together, talking easily.* **JOAN** *enters and joins them.*)

JOAN. I know what you two are talking about. That Per Se guy is a knockout!

CAROLINE. I'll say. I've never seen Bobby so excited by a guy.

HEIDI. She was smiling so much it was like an alien abduction.

FITNESS INSTRUCTOR. (*Recorded.*) All right ladies, it's Wednesday and this is Cardio Calorie Crunch.

(**LADIES** *cheer.*)

JOAN. So...what did we all think?

CAROLINE.

SO...

HEIDI.

SO...

JOAN.

SO?

ALL THREE.

SO!

CAROLINE.

SO THIS ONE'S COMPLICATED

HEIDI.

NOT LIKE THE OTHER MEN

JOAN.

AFTER ALL THE GUYS SHE'S DATED

CAROLINE.

THIS ONE'S SWEET

JOAN & CAROLINE.

AND SEPARATED

HEIDI.

DID YOU WATCH HER BOUNCE AROUND HIM?

JOAN.

COULD HER EYES LIGHT UP SOME MORE?

HEIDI.

SHE'S BEEN DIFFERENT SINCE SHE FOUND HIM

CAROLINE.

NEVER MAKES A PLAN WITHOUT HIM

ALL THREE.

SHE SAYS THEY'RE HAVING FUN

JOAN.

BUT THIS ONE

CAROLINE.

THIS ONE

ALL THREE.

THIS ONE COULD BE THE ONE

CAROLINE.

> DID YOU CATCH THE PART
> WHERE HE SAID SHE STOLE HIS HEART?

JOAN. I did.

CAROLINE & HEIDI.

> HE'S SMOOTH AND SMART

CAROLINE.

> LIKES FINE DINING AND FINE ART

HEIDI.

> HE'S A TRUE COUNTERPART

ALL THREE.

> A FRESH FACE FOR HER FRESH START
> MIGHT BE A MATCH
> MIGHT BE A MATCH
> IT SEEMS LIKE BOBBY MAY HAVE FOUND
> THE PERFECT CATCH

HEIDI.

> SO YOU KNOW PER SE SLEEPS OVER?

CAROLINE.

> SAYS HE STAYS THERE TWICE A WEEK

HEIDI.

> EVERY NIGHT SHE COOKS HIM DINNER

JOAN.

> BOBBY KNOWS SHE FOUND A WINNER

ALL THREE.

> EVERY GUY THAT CAME BEFORE HIM
> NEVER MADE HER ACT LIKE THIS
> EVERY DAY SHE LETS HIM MORE IN

HEIDI.

> MARK MY WORDS SHE'S FALLING FOR HIM

ALL THREE.

> LET'S NOT JUMP THE GUN
> IT COULD BE A FLING
> WE'LL WAIT FOR THE RING BUT

JOAN.

> THIS ONE

CAROLINE.
>THIS ONE

ALL THREE.
>THIS ONE
>HE IS THE ONE

FITNESS INSTRUCTOR. *(Recorded.)* All right ladies see you Monday for Brazilian Butt Burn.

CAROLINE.	**HEIDI.**	**JOAN.**
Shut up!	Go for it!	Boo!

>*(Scene: Bobby's loft.)*

>*(**PER SE** enters from the bedroom, putting on his shirt. **BOBBY** is cooking in the kitchen. He wraps his arms around her.)*

PER SE. Stop cooking. Let me take you out.

BOBBY. Not a chance. We've been out the last three nights.

PER SE. There is something about watching you eat your weight in lobster that I find so sexy.

BOBBY. Wait till you see how I eat frogs' legs. Now fix yourself a drink. Dinner in half an hour.

PER SE. What are we having?

BOBBY. Something new.

PER SE. It's always something new. It's been six months and you haven't repeated a single dinner.

BOBBY. What fun would that be?

PER SE. You know that's a little crazy.

BOBBY. But nice crazy, right?

PER SE. Most definitely. Now what delights are you serving me?

BOBBY. *(Flirting.)* Shaved Brussels sprout salad with grilled pears and pistachios followed by poached beef filet and smashed potatoes. Then a warm mixed berry shortcake with cream biscuits.

PER SE. You're spoiling me.

BOBBY. That's my pleasure.

(**BOBBY** *continues cooking and cuts herself badly.*)

BOBBY. Shit.

PER SE. (*Alarmed.*) Did you hurt yourself?

(**BOBBY** *examines the wound as* **PER SE** *rushes to her.*)

BOBBY. Damn.

PER SE. Let me see it.

BOBBY. I'm fine. The bleeding will stop soon. I just need a bandage.

(**BOBBY** *starts to exit.*)

PER SE. You must be in pain.

BOBBY. No, doesn't hurt at all.

(**PER SE** *looks at her skeptically.*)

Cooks cut themselves. It's a fact of life. Anyway give me a minute. Let me clean up and I'll finish cooking you dinner.

[MUSIC NO. 16 "WHAT MORE DO YOU NEED?"]

(*She tries to exit as he calls after her.*)

PER SE. Bobby, stop

BOBBY. No. I can take care of myself.

(**BOBBY** *exits offstage.*)

PER SE. Of course you can, but that's not the point.

I'VE BEEN THINKING
WELL... THERE'S ME
AND THERE'S YOU
AND THERE'S US
AND IT'S GREAT
I DIDN'T PLAN ON THIS
BUT I REALIZED TODAY...

(*A pause, while he gathers up the courage.* **BOBBY** *re-enters.*)

> MOVE IN WITH ME
> LET'S TAKE A LEAP
> I WANT TO BE THERE
>
> EACH NIGHT WHEN YOU SLEEP
> BOBBY, IT'S ME
> WHAT MORE DO YOU NEED?

BOBBY.

> I NEED TO CLEAN THE SHOWERHEAD

PER SE.

> DON'T MAKE JOKES

BOBBY.

> IT'S FILTHY
> IS IT BRIGHT IN HERE?

PER SE.

> DON'T TURN AWAY
> DON'T CLOSE OFF

BOBBY.

> I THINK I LEFT THE OVEN ON

PER SE.

> IT'S JUST A SURPRISE

BOBBY.

> I HATE SURPRISES

PER SE.

> IT'S JUST NEW

BOBBY.

> I LIKE MY LOFT

PER SE.

> GIVE ME THE CHANCE
> TO TAKE CARE OF YOU

BOBBY. *(Spoken, with realization.)* Take care of me...

PER SE & (BOBBY).

> MOVE IN WITH ME
> (DEFINE MOVE IN)
> LET'S BUILD A LIFE
> (LIKE, EVERY DAY TOGETHER?)
> LET'S DO IT NOW
> (LIKE EVERY NIGHT SPEND TOGETHER?)

WON'T IT BE NICE?
(YOU'D SHARE YOUR CLOSET SPACE WITH ME?)
BOBBY AND ME
WHAT MORE DO YOU NEED?

BOBBY.

I DON'T WANT TO SAIL ON A CRUISE.

PER SE. Who said anything about sailing on a cruise?

BOBBY.

THAT'S WHAT RETIRED COUPLES DO

PER SE. Retired? I didn't say…

BOBBY.

WHEN I FEEL LIKE I DON'T EVEN KNOW WHAT
I'M DOING MYSELF
LET'S TABLE THIS DISCUSSION
WE DON'T NEED TO RUSH IN
LET'S WAIT
LET'S DATE.

PER SE. *(Gently.)*

MOVE IN WITH ME
THERE'S NO TIME TO WASTE
YOU MAKE ME FEEL YOUNG
I'LL MAKE YOU FEEL SAFE,
BOBBY, WITH ME
WHAT MORE DO YOU NEED?

(They kiss. **PER SE** *exits.* **DEAD JIM** *enters.)*

DEAD JIM. You like him better than me?

*(***BOBBY** *is silent.)*

I don't want to be replaced by another man.

BOBBY. You never could be. This isn't about you.

DEAD JIM. I don't like that.

BOBBY. It's time to say goodbye.

DEAD JIM. Goodbye? Do you really mean that?

BOBBY. I do.

DEAD JIM. Will you change your mind?

*(***BOBBY** *shakes her head.)*

BOBBY. Goodbye, Jim.

    (**DEAD JIM** *exits.*)

    (*Scene transition:* **CAROLINE**, **HEIDI**, *and* **JOAN**
    enter into the living room as we hear the TV
    in the background.)

CAROLINE. (*Points remote.*) Why can't I get this thing to
    change channel?

BOBBY. Because it's not the cable clicker, Caroline.

    (**BOBBY** *hands* **CAROLINE** *the other clicker.*)

HEIDI. What is wrong with you?

JOAN. Completely inept in the face of modern technology.

CAROLINE. Don't knock my horse and buggy. Old Dobbin
    got me here and on time.

HEIDI. The program's starting – will you all be quiet?

JOAN. (*Grabbing the remote and turning off the TV.*) No.
    Bobby how is Per Se? Now there is a man... (*Barks/
    howls.*)

HEIDI. Definitely a keeper.

CAROLINE. If I wasn't married I'd be jealous.

BOBBY. There's been a development.

JOAN. Are you pregnant?

BOBBY. He wanted me to move in.

CAROLINE. And you said...?

    (**BOBBY** *indicates "no."*)

Now I know you're completely crazy.

HEIDI. He's perfect.

BOBBY. Sure...

JOAN. What happened?

BOBBY. (*Shrug.*) I suggested we take a break.

HEIDI. A break? Or a BREAK?

BOBBY. We'll see...

[MUSIC NO. 17 "WHY STOP HERE"]

JOAN. Bobby...

CAROLINE. Are you sure?

HEIDI. He could be your Prince Charming.

BOBBY. But I'm a work in progress.

> I COULD HAVE MOVED IN WITH HIM.
> I COULD HAVE SHARED HIS LIFE.
> AND MAYBE BECOME HIS WIFE
> I COULD HAVE TRIED
> INSTEAD I SAID GOODBYE

> I COULD HAVE MOVED IN WITH HIM
> I CERTAINLY HAD THE URGE
> TO SEE HOW OUR LIVES MIGHT MERGE
> IT COULD HAVE BEEN GOOD
> INSTEAD I'M STAYING PUT

> I'M NOT WORRIED
> I'M NOT BROKENHEARTED
> IT'S MY STORY AND I'VE ONLY STARTED

> I'LL POUR A GLASS
> AND RAISE A TOAST TO NEW BEGINNINGS
> DAY TO DAY AND YEAR TO YEAR
> I'LL JUST RELAX, I LIKE THE LIFE THAT I'M LIVING
> I NEVER THOUGHT I'D FEEL SO FREE, SO CLEAR
> WHY STOP HERE?

CAROLINE. Cheers!

> (**CAROLINE** *drinks.*)

BOBBY.
> WHY STOP HERE?

WOMEN.
> YOU COULD HAVE MOVED IN WITH HIM

JOAN.
> AND TAKEN A LEAP, A CHANCE

HEIDI.
> ON A HOLLYWOOD-STYLE ROMANCE

WOMEN.
> A FAIRYTALE END

BOBBY.

INSTEAD I'M WITH MY FRIENDS

(The **ENSEMBLE MEN** *enter variously.)*

MEN.

YOU COULD HAVE MOVED IN WITH HIM

DEAD JIM.

YOU COULD HAVE PAIRED AGAIN

PER SE.

WITH A DEBONAIR GENTLEMAN

SHRINK.

IT COULD HAVE GONE WELL

BOBBY.

INSTEAD I CHOSE MYSELF
AND TIME KEEPS MOVING
AND THE WORLD KEEPS TURNING
I FOUND MY GROOVE
AND NOW I'M ON MY JOURNEY

ALL.

POUR A GLASS
AND RAISE A TOAST TO NEW BEGINNINGS
DAY TO DAY AND YEAR TO YEAR
JUST RELAX
AND LIKE THE LIFE THAT YOU'RE LIVING

BOBBY.	**ENSEMBLE.**
I WON'T TURN BACK AND	OOH
WATCH IT DISAPPEAR	OOH

BOBBY.

I'LL GO ON VACATION
I'LL EAT DINNER IN BED
AND I'LL DATE IF I WANT OR I'LL FALL ASLEEP
WATCHING THE NEWS

WHEREVER I'M GOING,
I'M OKAY ON MY OWN
IT'S MY DECISION
IT'S MY DIRECTION
POINT IS: I CHOOSE

ALL.

> POUR A GLASS
> AND RAISE A TOAST TO NEW BEGINNINGS
> DAY TO DAY AND YEAR TO YEAR

ENSEMBLE.

> DAY TO DAY AND YEAR TO YEAR

ALL.

> JUST RELAX
> AND LIKE THE LIFE THAT YOU'RE LIVING

BOBBY.	**ENSEMBLE.**
I'VE COME THIS FAR,	OOH
THERE'S NOTHING LEFT TO FEAR	OOH

BOBBY.

> WHY STOP HERE?

WOMEN.

> WHY STOP HERE?

> *(The* **WOMEN** *exit.)*

SHRINK.

> WHY STOP HERE?

> *(The* **SHRINK** *exits.)*

PER SE.

> WHY STOP HERE?

> *(***PER SE** *exits.)*

> *(***BOBBY** *gives one last look to* **DEAD JIM**, *who
> smiles as he exits. She opens her laptop on the
> last beat of the song.)*

[MUSIC NO. 17A "CURVY WIDOW CURTAIN CALL"]

ENSEMBLE.

> CURVY WIDOW'S LICKING HER LIPS
> SHE'S SHAKING HER HIPS
> LOOK OUT ALL YOU MEN
> ACROSS THE WORLD WIDE WEB
> CURVY WIDOW'S GOT YOU IN HER SITES!

BOBBY.

THAT'S RIGHT

ENSEMBLE.

THAT'S RIGHT

ENSEMBLE & BOBBY.

CURVY WIDOW'S GOT YOU IN HER SITES!